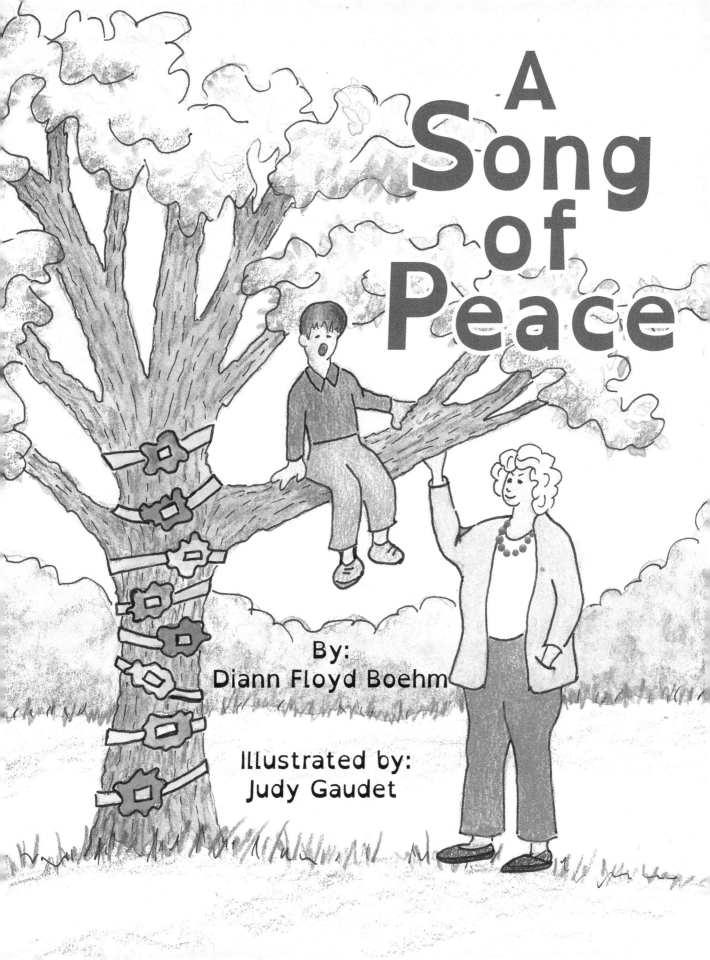

A Song of Peace

By:
Diann Floyd Boehm

Illustrated by:
Judy Gaudet

A Song of Peace

by Diann Floyd Boehm
illustrated by Judy Gaudet

Published by

Texas Sisters Press, LLC
www.TexasSistersPress.com

©2021 Diann Floyd Boehm

ISBN: 978-1-952041-53-2 (Hardcover)
ISBN: 978-1-952041-54-9 (Paperback)
ISBN: 978-1-952041-55-6 (Ebook)

One day in the park, a little boy named Tommy jumped off the merry-go-round. He stumbled a few steps and looked up at the sky.

Tommy walked over to a shady tree took a deep breath and sang, **"Peace, Peace, Peace."**

On a nearby bench, his mother looked up from her book, puzzled, as she listened to her son singing **"Peace."**

First, he sang the word **"Peace"** long and low, then short and fast: **"Peace."**

His neighbor, Mrs. Sills, walked by and asked the boy, "What are you doing?"

"I am singing the word, '**Peace**,'" the boy replied.

"Why?" Mrs. Sills asked curiously.

Tommy, looking surprised at the question, said simply, "Because the world needs it."

Mrs. Sills nodded her head in agreement.
Then, amazed by Tommy's wishes, she asked,
"How do you think this will help?"

Gazing up at his neighbor, Tommy explained,
"I started thinking . . . then I thought some more.
I just kept thinking about a way for **Peace** to
come to the world."

"My mom said it would be so lovely when there was finally **Peace** once more. So, I started thinking that if everyone thought about **Peace**, maybe it would come. I continued to think about it, but **Peace** did not come.

"While I was on the merry-go-round, I suddenly realized, I cannot just think about it; I have to say it or shout it or sing it! So now I am singing it!"

"Oh, and how will that help?" asked Mrs. Sills.

Tommy happily replied, "Maybe the angels will hear me."

With a baffled look, Mrs. Sills asked, "Why do you think the angels couldn't hear before?"

Tommy was delighted that Mrs. Sills wanted to understand, and so he explained.

Tommy shared how he thought the angels were tired of all the people fighting with one another. "I think the leaders are ignoring ideas that help to bring about **Peace**."

"I think the angels have given up on the grown-ups and have gone back home to rest."

"Do you think you can wake them up all by yourself?" Mrs. Sills asked.

ANGEL GARDEN

The little boy replied, "I don't know.
Maybe people will help. You could help!"

Mrs. Sills smiled and started singing, **"Peace."**

Tommy's mom came over, and she joined in, too

Little by little, more people joined in.

Then someone videoed them and, in an instant, they were on the internet.

Before they knew it, the word **"Peace"** was being sung nonstop in hundreds of languages worldwide.

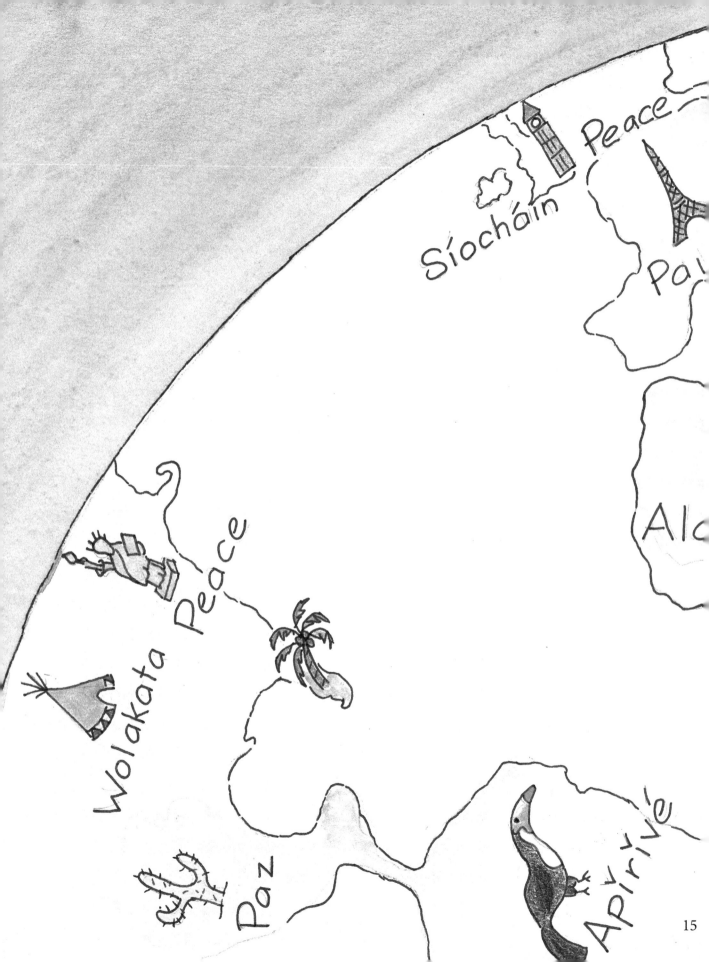

Síocháin

Peace

Pa

Al

Wolakata Peace

Paz

Apirive

Pace

Мир
Mir

Enx tajvan

Shalim
שלום
Salam
سلام

Héping

Shanti

Hotep

Santiphap

Amani

Vrede

16

Peace Peace Peace

Pretty soon, the animals in the forests and meadows heard the singing and joined in the chorus.

The birds seemed to sing louder as they flew about their day.

Fishermen saw dolphins jumping about, making sounds of joy as if singing **Peace** in their own little way.

Peace   Peace

Reports of singing started to come in from the most unusual places: the jungles, the ranches, and the Arctic and even Antarctica.

Sounds of love and softness filled the air, and the angels began to stir.

They listened to the song of "**Peace**" and believed the grown-ups were finally ready to have **Peace.**

Excited about this change, the angels got busy helping the world leaders see that **Peace** was possible.

The singing continued because, this time, people did not give up on **Peace**. Slowly **Peace** came to the earth.

But even so, Tommy kept singing **"Peace"**.

Others were puzzled when they heard that Tommy, his mom, and Mrs. Sills kept singing **Peace**.

Then one day, Tommy was singing in the front yard when a car drove up, and a man got out.

Tommy screamed, "Daddy! Daddy!" as he ran and jumped in his daddy's arms.

You see, Tommy sang **"Peace"** so that he could have his dad come home, and Tommy wanted all the other dads and moms to return home to their children, too!

AIR FORCE

When that happened, Tommy knew there was **Peace** in the world.

SEMPER PARATUS

1790

COAST GUARD

NAVY

MARINES

ARMY

The End.

About the Author
Diann Floyd Boehm

Diann is an author, educator, community volunteer, humanitarian, and former classroom teacher. Diann is passionate about storytelling. She is the author of seven books, some for younger children, some for YA and adults.

Her Little Girl in the Moon has delighted children all over the world. The Little Girl in the Moon Series is now The Moonling Adventures! The little boy in the moon and his dog Shadow are introduced in the Moonling Adventures – The Serengeti.

The Moonling Adventures – The Serengeti won "Best Texas Children's Book 2021". Harry the Camel was the number one children's bookseller in the B4R store!

https://www.diannfloydboehm.com/

About the Illustrator
Judy Gaudet

Judy Gaudet studied technical and medical illustration hoping to combine her career in microbiology with her lifelong love of art. Judy lives in southern Maine where she finds inspiration for her work in the landscapes, wildlife, and historic sites that surround her home.

Judy has illustrated two other children's books for author Cindi Flow - SandyBoy and His New Home and SandyBoy and The Christmas Blizzard.

CPSIA information can be obtained
at www.ICGtesting.com
Printed in the USA
BVHW021431121221
623842BV00002B/91